To Yuna.

Susanna Isern

To my little boy, who doesn't like that there are separate bathrooms for ladies and gents.

Gómez

É G A L I T È

Daniela the Pirate
Egalité Series

© Text: Susanna Isern, 2017
© Illustrations: Gómez, 2017
© Edition: NubeOcho, 2018
www.nubeocho.com - hello@nubeocho.com

Original title: *Daniela Pirata*
English translation: Ben Dawlatly
Text editing: Rebecca Packard

Distributed in the United States by
Consortium Book Sales & Distribution

First edition: 2018
ISBN: 978-84-17123-12-3

Printed in China by Asia Pacific Offset,
respecting international labor standards.

DANIELA
the PIRATE

SUSANNA ISERN
& GÓMEZ

nubeOCHO

IN A FARAWAY SEA

sailed the *Black Croc,* the most fearsome pirate ship of ALL TIME.

All other SEAFARING VESSELS planned their routes to stay well away from it, and if a sailor saw it through his SPYGLASS, he would spin his boat around and flee in the opposite direction.

The captain of the BLACK CROC was called CHOPPYLOBE. He and all his fearsome men were famous for their bone-chilling adventures.

DANIELA was also sailing in those distant waters aboard her small sailboat, the JUMPING SPIDER.

Despite the horrible tales people told, she was in search of that TERRIFYING SHIP. There was something that she wanted more than anything else in the world:

Daniela wanted to be a PIRATE on the BLACK CROC!

One day, after many a sun and moon
had risen and set while SEARCHING,

SHE FOUND IT.

"My name is Daniela and
I WANT TO BE A PIRATE
on your ship!"

"Did that **LITTLE GIRL** just say she wanted to join
our crew?" asked a shocked Choppylobe.
"That's right!" answered Daniela decisively.

The pirates fell about **LAUGHING**.

The captain called his MEN into a huddle.
After several minutes of hushed discussion,
Choppylobe spoke:

"To be a pirate on the *Black Croc* you need to pass a series of TESTS."

"Tests? I'LL DO WHATEVER IT TAKES!" said Daniela confidently.

"The FIRST TEST you have to pass to be a pirate is to catch a whole load of fish. Little girl, DO YOU KNOW HOW TO FISH?"

DANIELA DOVE
INTO THE SEA.

"HERE YOU HAVE a few pounds of sea bass, some prawns, three giant squids and a manta ray."

When she came back, the pirates were DUMBSTRUCK.

"Not bad..." Choppylobe admitted. "The SECOND TEST you have to pass to be a pirate is to prove that you have the strength of a sturdy oak. Little girl, ARE YOU STRONG?"

Daniela picked up the heavy treasure chest, threw it onto her shoulders and started to BEND HER KNEES. The pirates looked on speechless.

"One, two! Ten squats! Twenty! Fifty! A HUNDRED SQUATS!"

"The THIRD TEST you have to pass to be a pirate is to run at the speed of lightning. Little girl, ARE YOU FAST?"

Daniela **DARTED** around the deck. A couple of seconds later she came to a halt in front of the astonished salty seadogs.

"Look! The eyepatch from Old Blinky, a feather from your parrot and a gold doubloon. I've taken them off you **SO QUICK** you didn't even notice."

"**GIVE ME MY COIN BACK!**" Choppylobe was getting annoyed.

"The **FOURTH TEST** you have to pass to be a pirate is to be as stealthy as a snake. Little girl, **CAN YOU MOVE SILENTLY?**"

Daniela jumped in her sailboat and headed off. The next morning she turned up smiling with a **TUFT OF FUR** between her fingers. The pirates rubbed their eyes in disbelief.

"A lock of hair from the **TERRIBLE BEAR**. He was sleeping in his cave, and I cut this off without waking him."

"Let me see..." The dumbfounded Choppylobe examined it.

"The **FIFTH TEST** you have to pass to be a pirate is to prove that you're not scared of anything.
Little girl, **ARE YOU BRAVE?**"

Daniela jumped into the CROCODILE PIT. When they saw how bold she was, the reptiles froze with fear. The scurvy-ridden seafarers looked at her with ADMIRATION.

"The RUSTY KEY from the bottom of the pit. I bet it's been down there for months, years perhaps, waiting for somebody brave enough to fetch it."

"Bring me the key." The captain took it off her as he started to get nervous.

"The SIXTH TEST you have to pass to be a pirate is to prepare a great soup. Little girl, DO YOU KNOW HOW TO COOK?"

Daniela grabbed the TASTIEST INGREDIENTS: spider webs, frogspawn, crocodile tears and a rotten coconut, and she prepared a SUCCULENT SOUP.

"The most disgusting soup you've ever tried!"

"Yuck... marvelously repugnant!" said Choppylobe licking his lips.
"But, THE MOST IMPORTANT TEST you have to pass to be a pirate
is finding hidden treasure. Little girl, CAN YOU READ THIS MAP?"

Daniela STUDIED the treasure map that had puzzled the pirates for months. She sailed away on the *Jumping Spider.* Two days later, she returned with the plunder. It was a huge TREASURE BOX full of valuable jewels and gold coins.

The pirates could not believe their eyes. They were so happy that they raised Daniela up onto their shoulders and tossed her in the air while CHEERING her name.

"Ahem... there's no doubt you've passed all the tests..." grumbled the captain.
"But... no... YOU CAN'T BE A PIRATE on our ship."

"What? WHY NOT? I can CATCH tons of fish, I'm as STRONG as an oak, as FAST as lightning, as SNEAKY as a snake, I'm BRAVE, I'm awful at COOKING and I can find hidden TREASURES...

"I'M THE FULL PACKAGE!"

"It's very simple," said Choppylobe. "You're missing the most important requirement. You can't be a PIRATE because YOU'RE A GIRL, and only BOYS are allowed on this ship. It's a rule on the *Black Croc*."

When she heard those ridiculous words, DANIELA WAS SPEECHLESS. And if she didn't find it so hard to cry, she would have filled the sea with tears.

Then the pirates formed another huddle, but this time they left out Choppylobe, who COULD NOT BELIEVE what was happening.

After some minutes of discussion, a spokesperson said:

"Daniela has shown that she has what it takes TO BE A PIRATE. We want her to stay on the ship."

"AYE! SHE'S STAYING!" they all shouted.

Daniela started to jump while hugging the pirates.

CHOPPYLOBE, on the other hand, had turned as red as a lobster. He looked like a pressure cooker that was ABOUT TO EXPLODE.

"How dare you make a decision like that without consulting me, you rabble of ruffians!
I'M THE CAPTAIN!" he screamed.

"Choppylobe, to be captain you have to have certain qualities. The most important one is BEING FAIR, and if you don't want Daniela just because she's a girl, well that's just not fair."

"WE WANT YOU TO LEAVE!"

CHOPPYLOBE DISAPPEARED,

and nobody ever heard from him again.

And the BLACK CROC charted new courses around THE WHOLE WORLD.

They say that all other seafaring vessels planned their routes to stay well away from it, and if a SAILOR saw the scary ship through his SPYGLASS, he would turn his boat around and flee in the opposite direction.

Everyone knew that CHOPPYLOBE was not the captain of the *Black Croc* anymore...

The new captain of the ship was a girl,
DANIELA THE PIRATE.